A Place for MULAN

DISNEY

Written by **MARIE CHOW**

Illustrated by **JASPER SHAW**

For Tycho, Athena, and Zora
—M.C.

For my parents, whose love and support
have allowed me to pursue my dreams
—J.S.

Published by Disney Press, an imprint of Disney Book Group.

Printed in the United States of America

First Hardcover Edition, February 2020

1 3 5 7 9 10 8 6 4 2

ISBN 978-1-368-02348-1

Library of Congress Control Number: 2019940218

FAC-034274-19361

Designed by Soyoung Kim

For more Disney Press fun, visit www.disneybooks.com

MULAN was a girl
who never behaved
the way people expected.

She was a spirited girl.
Some might say *too* spirited.

Sometimes she didn't fit in
with what was expected at home.

And Mulan didn't exactly
fit in with the other girls
in her village, either.

She wasn't
careful or quiet.

She was rarely
graceful.

And she was almost
never refined.

Mulan didn't fit in with the chickens.

Because, well, she wasn't a chicken.

Mulan's mother found it difficult to explain why Mulan was . . . the way she was.

"Mulan," her mother would say, "I need you to at least *try* to behave."

"I do try," Mulan said.

"Then please try harder."

So when Mulan practiced calligraphy, she tried her very hardest.

Mulan listened intently while her father explained the proper way to make brushstrokes.

But eventually, she found
herself staring at the sky.

"Father, have you ever noticed that our brushstrokes look like the neck of a crane? Graceful and strong."

Mulan's father smiled . . . and then redirected Mulan to the task at hand.

Paying attention was difficult.

After a while, Mulan found new uses for her calligraphy brush . . . and her parents were not amused.

"Mulan, there is a time and place for warriors. But now is not that time, and this is not that place," her father said.

Later that day, Mulan visited
the horses in the courtyard.
Her favorite was Black Wind.

She enjoyed taking care of him . . .

. . . and she especially loved to ride.

There was nothing better than the feeling of the wind in her hair as Black Wind galloped through the lush countryside.

Riding was Mulan's one comfort.

But she wondered if the day would ever come when she'd find a place to belong.

When Mulan returned home, it was time for weaving. She watched as her little sister did it effortlessly.

"Xiu, you make your ancestors proud," her mother said.

Mulan tried . . . .

but couldn't quite . . .

figure it out.

Xiu helped clean up. "You're fighting the materials instead of working with them."

Mulan's sister untangled the fabric.

"Take this piece," Xiu said. "You're trying to make it something it doesn't want to be."

"I've been doing a lot of that lately," Mulan said, sighing.

In the back of the room, their father cleared his throat. "Xiu is very wise."

He invited Mulan to go for a walk.

As soon as they got outside,
Mulan cried, "I try so hard
to be like everyone else!"

"I know," her father said.

"But I don't belong. And the harder
I try, the less I fit in," she said.

Mulan's father pointed to a meadow
full of yellow flowers.

"Mulan, see how these flowers fit together?
When they're in a field, it's difficult to tell
them apart."

A tear ran down Mulan's cheek.
"I would give anything to be like them."

"But what if you are not a yellow flower,
Mulan?" He motioned to a nearby tree.
"What if you are a magnolia blossom?

"No matter how hard she tries,
a magnolia will always be what she is:
beautiful, distinct . . . and different."

Mulan's father continued. "You jump in puddles because you are adventuresome.

"You twirl your brushes because you see possibilities others don't.

"You ride horses because you are spirited and brave."

Mulan's heart swelled.

She felt her sadness melt away.
She wasn't the same as everyone else . . .
but Mulan had gifts of her own.

Mulan knew her path would be
different . . . and for the first time,
different didn't feel so bad.